Young Princesses
AROUND THE WORLD

Elizabeth and the Royal Pony

Based on a True Story of Elizabeth I of England

BY JOAN HOLUB • ILLUSTRATED BY NONNA ALESHINA

READY-TO-READ • ALADDIN

NEW YORK   LONDON   TORONTO   SYDNEY

This book is a work of historical fiction based on the author's careful research. Dialogue and events are the product of the author's imagination, and any resemblance to actual events or persons, living or dead, is entirely coincidental.

ALADDIN PAPERBACKS
An imprint of Simon & Schuster Children's Publishing Division
1230 Avenue of the Americas, New York, NY 10020
Text copyright © 2007 by Joan Holub
Illustrations copyright © 2007 by PiArt & Design Agency
All rights reserved, including the right of reproduction in whole
or in part in any form.
READY-TO-READ is a registered trademark of Simon & Schuster, Inc.
ALADDIN PAPERBACKS and colophon are trademarks of Simon & Schuster, Inc.
Also available in an Aladdin library edition.
Designed by Karin Paprocki
The text of this book was set in Century Oldstyle BT.
Manufactured in the United States of America
First Aladdin Paperbacks edition March 2007
2 4 6 8 10 9 7 5 3 1
Library of Congress Cataloging-in-Publication Data
Holub, Joan.
Elizabeth and the royal pony : a true story of Elizabeth I of England /
by Joan Holub ; illustrated by Nonna Aleshina.—1st ed.
p. cm.—(Ready-to-read) (Young princesses around the world ; #1)
ISBN-13: 978-0-689-87191-7 (pbk.)   ISBN-10: 0-689-87191-0 (pbk.)
ISBN-13: 978-0-689-87193-1 (lib. bdg.)   ISBN-10: 0-689-87193-7 (lib. bdg.)
1. Elizabeth I, Queen of England, 1533–1603—Juvenile. I. Aleshina, Nonna. II. Title.
III. Series. IV. Series: Holub, Joan. Young princesses around the world ; #1.
DA355.H63 2007   942.05'5092—dc22   [B]   2006010103

For Elizabeth Ensley

1

Elizabeth and the Royal Pony

The wind blew through Princess Elizabeth's long red hair as she rode toward the forest.

"Faster, Pegasus," she told her golden pony. Pegasus galloped across the grass, taking her away from the palace. Behind her, Elizabeth heard the pounding hooves of the ponies her brother and sister rode.

"Slow down, Elizabeth!" her younger brother, Edward, shouted.

Nine-year-old Elizabeth laughed and rode faster.

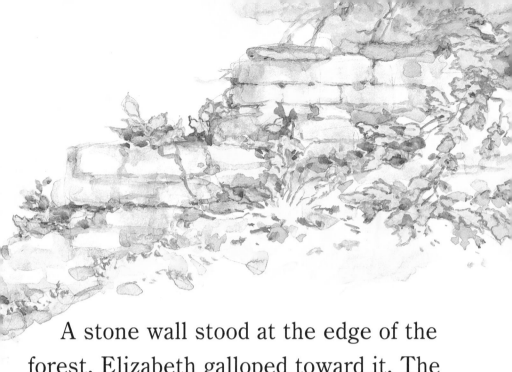

A stone wall stood at the edge of the forest. Elizabeth galloped toward it. The closer they got to the wall, the more worried she became. What if her pony would not jump over it?

"Jump, Pegasus!" she whispered.

A few feet from the wall, her pony's eyes grew scared. He snorted wildly and suddenly reared on his hind legs.

Elizabeth felt herself slipping.

"Help!"

With a jolt, Pegasus threw her out of the saddle.

Elizabeth stood up and brushed the dirt from her skirt. She had fallen in soft grass, but she still felt sore.

Pegasus pawed the ground nearby, looking ashamed.

She rubbed his nose. "It's all right. I am not mad at you."

Elizabeth watched Prince Edward and her older sister, Princess Mary, ride toward her. Beyond them was Hatfield, the palace where they all lived with their servants.

Their father was Henry VIII, the king of England. He lived miles away, in one of his many big castles near London.

Edward hopped off his pony
when he reached Elizabeth.

"Are you hurt?" he asked her.

Elizabeth shook her head.
"No. Pegasus and I shall try again
another day."

"Father would be proud of your
bravery," said Edward.

Elizabeth smiled at him. But she knew the truth. Because she was a girl, her father would never really be proud of her. Edward had always been her father's favorite. Only boys could become kings, so Edward would be crowned king when their father died someday.

"Pegasus should be whipped for throwing you," said Mary as she rode up to them.

"No!" said Elizabeth. She stroked her pony's mane. "Punishing him won't help."

"Beat him, or you will never make him jump," said Mary. "He will break your neck first."

But Elizabeth knew she would not do what Mary suggested. "I cannot force Pegasus to follow my orders. Somehow I must teach him to trust me enough that he will jump."

"How will you do that?" asked Edward.

"I am not sure. I think I need more advice," said Elizabeth.

CHAPTER 2

Elizabeth Gets Advice

Back at the palace the royal children left their ponies at the stables. Grooms hurried out to unsaddle them.

Elizabeth went to speak to the stable master.

"Pegasus will not jump over the stone wall," she told him. "I have tried it with him many times."

The stable master thought for a moment. "A pony will not jump if he is not feeling well. I will find out if he is hurt or sick."

Elizabeth watched as he felt Pegasus's legs and sides. He checked the pony's hooves for stones and splinters.

"Pegasus is fine," the stable master told Elizabeth.

"Then why won't he jump?" she asked.

"Perhaps the stone wall is too high for his first jump. Begin with something lower and easier," he suggested. He laid a long stick on the ground.

"That is *too* easy. Even I could jump over a stick!" said Elizabeth.

"Succeeding at an easy jump will make Pegasus feel sure of his ability. As he becomes more confident, he will try harder jumps," said the stable master.

"That sounds like good advice," said Elizabeth. "I will think about it."

Elizabeth went into the palace and
upstairs to the study. Kat, the lady who
had been her governess since she was
three years old, sat in the corner sewing.

Kat had come to take care of her after Elizabeth's mother, Queen Anne Boleyn, was beheaded. Elizabeth shivered. She didn't like to think about her mother's death.

"Did you enjoy your ride?" Kat asked her.

Elizabeth sighed. "Pegasus still won't jump. If you were trying to teach him, what would you do?"

Kat smiled and shrugged. "I don't know anything about horses."

"But you are a good teacher," said Elizabeth. "How did you teach me to read, write, dance, and play the lute?"

Kat poked her needle in and out, sewing with blue thread. "You were easy to teach. You wanted to please me, so you did what I told you."

"I think Pegasus wants to please me. But he still won't jump," said Elizabeth.

"Perhaps you should give him a treat each time he performs a hard task. That way he will know you are pleased," said Kat.

"That sounds like good advice," said Elizabeth. "I will think about it."

The next day Elizabeth led Pegasus
from his stable.

She laid a long stick on the ground
as the stable master had suggested.
She mounted Pegasus and walked him
toward it.

"See that stick? It is much lower than
the stone wall. Step over it, Pegasus,"
she said.

Pegasus stepped over the stick.

Elizabeth slid off his back and gave him a bite of apple.

He munched it happily.

Next she led Pegasus to a log that lay on the ground nearby.

"Let's try something a little harder," she told him.

She sat on her pony's back and walked him toward the log. He stepped over it. She gave him another bite of apple.

The next day Pegasus jumped over a low fence. Elizabeth was delighted. He had never jumped so high before.

They practiced jumping over the low fence for two weeks. After each jump Elizabeth rewarded Pegasus with a treat.

"Now it is time to try a really hard jump," Elizabeth told Pegasus one day. They rode across the grass toward the forest. Elizabeth leaned low against her pony's mane and headed toward the stone wall. This time perhaps Pegasus would really jump it!

But the closer they got to the wall,
the more worried she became. She
did not want to fall again.

At the last minute Pegasus stopped
in front of the wall. He reared in
fright. Princess Elizabeth fell to the
ground.

She got up slowly and walked over
to pat her pony's neck. "It's all right,
Pegasus. One day we will fly over the
wall together. I know it!"

They galloped back to Hatfield.

CHAPTER 3

Elizabeth Takes a Trip

When Elizabeth reached the palace, Edward ran toward her, waving a letter.

"King Henry has written to tell us he is getting married!" he shouted.

Again? This would be his sixth wife! But Elizabeth did not dare say such a thing aloud. No one was allowed to question the king's decisions. Her mother had learned that the hard way.

"He is going to marry a lady named Catherine Parr," Edward said. "And he wants us to attend the wedding!"

"Me too?" asked Elizabeth.

Edward smiled. "All of us. You, Mary, and me."

Elizabeth and Edward rushed inside to pack. It was a great honor to be invited to visit the king.

A week later the royal children left for London with many servants.

Elizabeth, Edward, and Mary rode on fancy mattresses called litters. Strong horses and oxen carried them along.

Pegasus and the other ponies trotted behind them.

The king's castle was only thirty miles away, but it felt like farther. The dirt roads on the way to the castle were rutted and muddy. Their journey was slow.

Edward slept during most of the trip. Mary stayed hidden behind the curtains around her litter.

Elizabeth often rode Pegasus instead of sitting on her litter. She waved to the villagers and farmers as she passed them. She wanted the English people to know she cared about them.

The people enjoyed her interest. They waved back to her and shouted kind words. Children brought her gifts of flowers they had picked in the fields.

Elizabeth Goes to a Wedding

After days of travel they reached King Henry's castle. His wedding would take place the next morning.

They found the king in his court talking with important people. Elizabeth noticed that everyone listened to his ideas and opinions. They trusted his wisdom and leadership.

But no one was allowed to speak to the king unless he spoke to them first. Not even a princess. So the royal children waited.

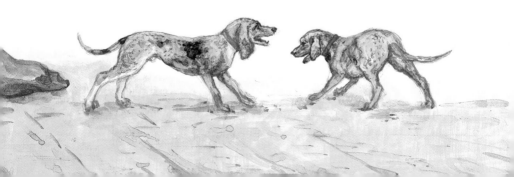

The king called his three children closer when he saw them. First he spoke to Edward for a while. Then he spoke to Mary.

Finally he waved Elizabeth forward.

Princess Elizabeth tripped as she walked toward the throne.

The king laughed. "Are you afraid of your own father?"

"No. I'm—," began Elizabeth.

"Perhaps she is a coward like her pony," teased Mary.

"Mary thinks Pegasus is a coward, but he isn't," Elizabeth explained to her father. "I am trying to teach him to trust me enough to jump over a stone wall."

"To earn your pony's trust, you must make him think you are a confident leader," the king advised her. "Even if you are unsure, do not let him know. If he

senses that you doubt your abilities as a
rider, he will doubt his ability to jump."

"Thank you, Father," said Elizabeth.
"That sounds like very good advice. I
will think about it."

The next day King Henry and
Catherine Parr were married at the palace.
Afterward they left on a wedding trip.

Elizabeth, Edward, and Mary
followed their father and his new
bride down the path on their ponies.
They threw flowers and waved.

Suddenly, something fell from the royal litter. It tumbled down a hill and around a rock wall. No one noticed except Elizabeth.

"The queen has dropped her silk fan!" she told Pegasus. "We must get it for her!"

Elizabeth steered Pegasus off the path and rode toward the wall. She showed her pony where she wanted him to go by pressing her knees to his sides and tugging on his reins.

The rock wall was as tall as the stone wall back at Hatfield. Would Pegasus refuse to jump over it and throw her off once again?

As they neared the wall, Elizabeth remembered to stay calm so her pony would trust her. She leaned over his mane.

"Fly, Pegasus!" she whispered. "We can do it."

Pegasus lifted his forelegs. They sailed over the rock wall.

Pegasus had jumped!

When they landed on the other side, Elizabeth hopped to the ground. She grabbed the fan and mounted Pegasus once again. They rode swiftly back to the queen.

The queen thanked her, and the king smiled. "Well done, Elizabeth!" he said.

Elizabeth hugged Pegasus as they rode back to Edward and Mary. "Good boy," she told him.

Together they had made her father proud.

"I hope I have a beautiful wedding someday," said Mary as they watched the king and queen ride away.

Elizabeth thought of her mother, who had been beheaded on the king's orders years ago.

"I will never marry," she said.

"Don't be silly. Princesses have to marry princes who will lead their countries," said Mary.

"Girls can be leaders, just like boys," said Elizabeth.

Edward and Mary laughed at her.

Elizabeth just smiled. She knew that someday she would prove it.

CHAPTER

5

Queen Elizabeth

Elizabeth grew up to be one of the most powerful queens in England's history. She chose smart people to be in her government. She listened to their advice, then tried to make good decisions.

Everyone wanted Elizabeth to get married so England would have a king. She refused because she didn't want to give up any of her power.

During her reign great art, music, and books were created. She encouraged trade and exploration, and sent settlers to America.

The English people trusted Elizabeth and were proud of her confidence and steady leadership. They nicknamed her Good Queen Bess.

This time line lists important events in Elizabeth's life:

1533   She is born the daughter of England's King Henry VIII and Queen Anne Boleyn on September 7. Her parents are disappointed that she is not a boy.

1536   Her mother is beheaded on the king's orders. Elizabeth is sent to live away from his castle.

1547   King Henry VIII dies after ruling England for thirty-eight years. Her half brother, Edward VI, becomes the king at age nine.

1553   Edward VI dies from illness, probably tuberculosis.

1553   Her older half sister, Mary I, becomes Queen of England.

1554   Elizabeth is suspected of plotting to have Mary killed. She is jailed in the Tower of London for two months.

1558   Mary dies from an unknown illness. Elizabeth becomes queen of England at age twenty-five.

1559   Elizabeth becomes head of the Church of England.

1562   She nearly dies from an illness called smallpox.

1581   She knights English explorer Francis Drake after he sails around the world.

1585   Settlers establish the first English colony in America on Roanoke Island, North Carolina.

1587   Elizabeth's cousin, Mary Queen of Scots, is executed for plotting to kill her.

1588   England's navy defeats the invading Spanish Armada in a sea battle.

1599   The Globe Theatre, where many of William Shakespeare's plays will be performed, opens in England.

1600   The East India Company is formed to expand England's trade with Asia.

1603   Elizabeth dies on March 24, at age sixty-nine, after ruling for forty-four years. Her tomb is in beautiful Westminster Abbey in London, England.

Joan Holub is the author of more than eighty books for children. She lives in Seattle, Washington.

Nonna Aleshina lives in Russia.

READY-TO-READ

LEVEL 3

Princess Elizabeth

of England is trying to teach her golden pony to jump over a stone wall—but no matter what she tries, he won't budge! After seeking advice from people in the kingdom, the princess finally asks her father, King Henry VIII, for help. And what he says just might help her navigate more than a stone wall.

Ready-to-Read books offer children a world of possibilities at four different reading levels:

PRE-LEVEL 1

Recognizing Words

- Word repetition
- Familiar words and phrases
- Simple sentences

LEVEL 1

Starting to Read

- Simple stories
- Increased vocabulary
- Longer sentences

LEVEL 2

Reading Independently

- More-complex stories
- Varied sentence structure
- Paragraphs and short chapters

LEVEL 3

Reading Proficiently

- Rich vocabulary
- More-challenging stories
- Longer chapters

Ready for more? Look for Ready-for-Chapters books.

A Ready-to-Read Book/Fiction
ALADDIN PAPERBACKS
Simon & Schuster, New York
Cover designed by Karin Paprocki
Cover illustration copyright © 2007 by Nonna Aleshina
Ages 6–8
www.SimonSaysKids.com
0307

US $3.99 / $4.99 CAN
ISBN-13: 978-0-689-87191-7
ISBN-10:   0-689-87191-0

EAN

9 780689 871917

50399

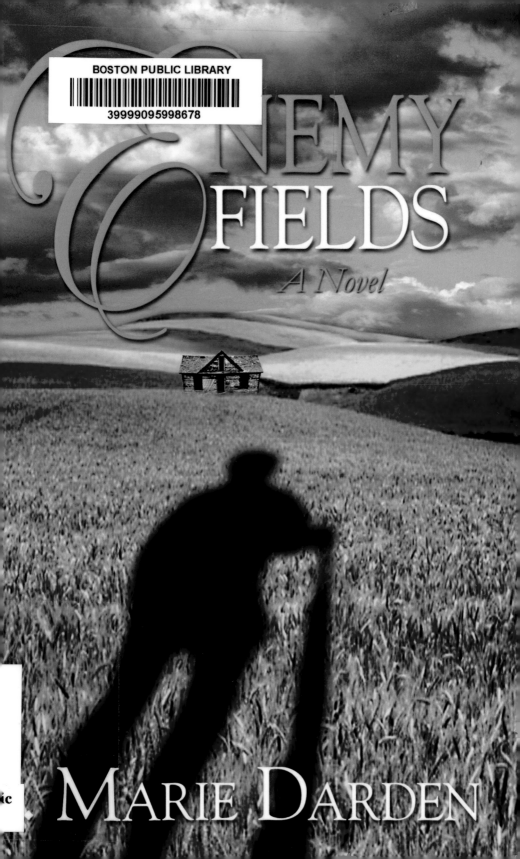

ENEMY FIELDS

A Novel

MARIE DARDEN